CAROUSEL

Brian Wildsmith

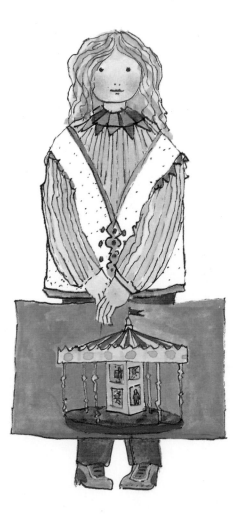

Oxford University Press
Oxford Toronto Melbourne

The fair was coming at last. Every year it visited the little town where Rosie and her brother Tom lived.

As the lorries came nearer, all the children ran out of the town and stood by the roadside. They all waved to welcome the fair.

As dusk fell, the fair drove into town and the children cheered with joy.

When they went to bed that night, they were so excited that they could hardly sleep.

The next day the children watched while the fair was set up.

Then when all was ready, Rosie and Tom raced to the Carousel because this was their favourite ride.

Around and around they went. 'I wish I could ride this Carousel for ever,' shouted Rosie.

But after a few days the fair moved on to another town, and the children were sad. 'Don't forget to come back next year,' called Rosie.

That winter Rosie became very ill, and the doctor came to see her.

He examined Rosie carefully and then told Tom and his parents she would have to stay in bed for a long, long time.

Spring came but Rosie was still sick. 'She is very sad,'
the doctor told her parents. 'But keep on telling her that
she will get better in time. You must give her hope.'

Tom overheard what the doctor said. And he had an idea.

He went to see Rosie's friends. 'It's Rosie's birthday tomorrow and she is so sad. We must cheer her up.' They all threw a coin in the fountain and made a wish.

Then Tom took his savings from his money-box and went to the toy-shop.

The next afternoon all Rosie's friends came to see her.
Each of them had drawn a picture for her.

'Happy Birthday, Rosie,' they all said. 'Please get well soon.'

'Oh, what beautiful paintings,' said Rosie.
'All my favourite rides on the Carousel – the Snowflake,
the Wings of Time, the Kangaroo . . .

'. . . and there's the Story-chair, the Unicorn, and the Throne.
Oh, how I wish I could ride on them all right now.'

Then Tom gave Rosie his present. It was a little Carousel that went round and round and played a pretty tune.

That night Rosie had a high temperature. 'If only I could ride on the Carousel,' she thought as she fell asleep.

As her eyes closed,
Rosie heard the Carousel say:

*'Step aboard and we will fly
through the window, through the sky . . .'*

Swinging, swinging to and fro
in a land of ice and snow.

With snowflakes falling everywhere,
her fever fell in the cold night air.

Then she rode the Wings of Time,
listened to their soothing rhyme:
'Doctors come and doctors go,
but Time is the best medicine I know.'

On she went, up through the air,
riding on the Story-chair.

To meet the friends from
books she'd read
each night as she lay
ill in bed.

Safe aboard the Kangaroo,
through the moonlit night she flew.

In splendour she was carried high,

up and up into the sky,

towards the moon,
all shining bright,

on that magic, starry night.

The Milky Way streams out afar
– catch the light, and catch your star.

Through space and time,
rushing, falling . . .

Then Bump! She awoke, sprawled on the floor beside her bed.

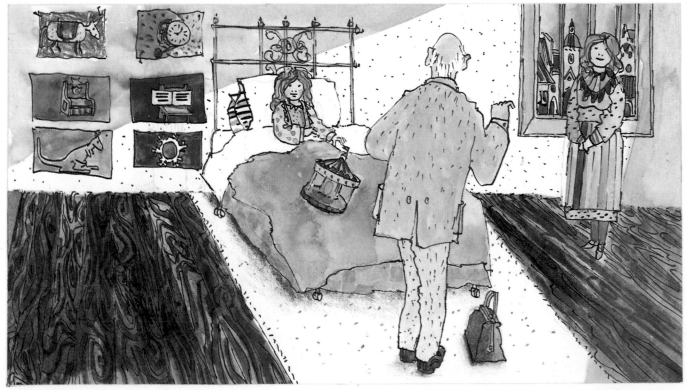

The doctor came back to see her. 'Good heavens, Rosie, your temperature has fallen and you look so much better,' he said.

As the days passed, Rosie got stronger and stronger.
The doctor came for the last time and told her she was
really better now and could go outside.

Tom rushed out to tell Rosie's friends and they all waited
outside to welcome her . . . and at that moment the fair
came back to town.

When the fair was set up,
Tom and Rosie raced to the
Carousel. Rosie had a ride
on everything.

'Thank you, Carousel,'
she said. 'Thank you.'